I HATE CAMPING

I HATE CAMPING

by P. J. Petersen

illustrated by
Frank Remkiewicz

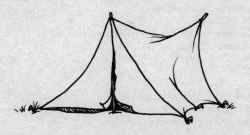

DUTTON CHILDREN'S BOOKS
NEW YORK

Library of Congress Cataloging-in-Publication Data

Petersen, P. J.
  I hate camping / by P. J. Petersen; illustrated by Frank
Remkiewicz.—1st ed.
      p. cm.
  Summary: Dan thinks he is going to have a terrible time
when he is forced to go camping with his mother's boyfriend
Mike and Mike's brainy son Raymond, but the two boys
form a surprising friendship.
  ISBN 0-525-44673-7
  [1. Camping—Fiction. 2. Friendship—Fiction.]
I. Remkiewicz, Frank, ill. II. Title.
PZ7.P44197Iad 1991   90-39650
[E]—dc20   CIP
                                                 AC

Published in the United States by
Dutton Children's Books,
a division of Penguin Books USA Inc.

Designer: Susan Phillips

Printed in U.S.A.

Reprinted by arrangement with Dutton Children's Books, a division of
Penguin Books USA Inc.
10 9 8 7 6 5 4 3 2 1

for Marian—for obvious reasons

P.J.P.

for Kendra

F.R.

Chapter 1

I was lying in front of the TV, drawing pictures of race cars. Mom came through the front door with a bag of groceries and said, "I have a surprise for you."

"Oh, no," I said. Mom's surprises are never ice cream or candy or a new video game. Her surprises are jobs or hard books or some kind of lessons.

"Mike is going to take you camping." Mom calls Mike her special friend. That just means Mike is Mom's boyfriend. He wants to marry her, but she's not sure yet.

"No, thank you," I said. "I hate camping."

"How can you hate camping? You've never tried it."

"I went camping with the Boys' Club," I said. "And it rained. And the mosquitoes ate us up. And the bus got a flat tire."

"That was a long time ago," Mom said.

"I still remember every bit of it," I said. "Johnny Black got poison oak, and another kid got sick—"

Mom waved for me to stop. "All right. That was a bad trip. But this one will be different. Camping can be fun if you do it right."

"I still don't want to go."

"It'll be good for you," she said. "You're turning into a tube toad."

"A what?"

"A tube toad. All you do is lie there like a toad and watch TV."

"That's what summers are for," I said.

Mom smiled. "I thought summers were for walking in the sunshine and reading special books and doing art projects and helping mothers."

"That was in the old days," I said. "Now summers are for sleeping late and watching TV and going to Star World." Star World is an amusement park north of the city. I love it, but Mom hates the crowds.

"Help me put away the groceries," Mom said.

I got up and looked into the bag. Broccoli. Tomatoes. Beans. "You forgot the candy bars and chips," I said. That was a joke. Mom *never* buys things like that.

Mom handed me the milk carton. "Mike's taking you to Baker Lake."

I put the milk in the refrigerator. "Do I have to go? I hate camping. You drive all day to get there. You eat burned food. The bugs bite you. You have to sleep on the hard ground. Then the ants come crawling into your sleeping bag. And the frogs. And the snakes. Who needs it?"

"Wait until you see Baker Lake," Mom said. "It's beautiful there."

"It's beautiful right here," I told her. "We ought to camp here."

Mom started handing me vegetables. "Oh, sure."

"Why not? The carpet's nice and soft for sleeping. And we have a TV. And the weather's just right. When we get hungry, we can call out for a pizza."

"You'll have a good time," Mom said. "Kim and Raymond are going." Kim and Raymond are Mike's kids.

I closed the refrigerator. "Now I *really* don't want to go," I said. "That little Kim talks all the time, and Raymond hates me."

Mom shook her head. "Give them a chance. This trip will be a good way for you to get to know them."

"I already know them. That's the trouble."

Mom folded the grocery bag and put it under the sink. "Just wait. You'll have a good time."

"Come on, Mom. You can talk Mike out of this. This is a horrible idea. Tell him to take us to Star World. Or a movie. Or a baseball game. We don't want to go camping."

"You'll have a good time," she said again.

"Mom, you know Raymond. His idea of a good time is reading the encyclopedia. Can you see him camping?"

Mom looked straight at me. "Mike has everything planned, and you're going."

I walked back to the living room. "Have you heard about the bears this year?" I said. "They're all over the place."

"You're going," Mom said.

"People have been feeding the bears too much. Now the bears come right down into the camps. They knock over tents and—"

"You're going."

"My stomach hurts," I said. "I think I'm coming down with something."

6

"You're still going."

"I just hope there isn't a forest fire," I began. But I knew it was no use.

Chapter 2

Mom woke me at six the next morning. "Mike wants to get an early start," she said.

"What's the hurry?" I asked. "We can go late, and the bears will still be there. And the snakes. And the mosquitoes. And the bats."

Mom checked my bag to be sure I had everything. "Put in your toothbrush," she said.

"The bears don't care if my teeth are clean," I said.

As soon as she left the room, I opened my bag. I put in my tape player and my earphones and six cassette tapes. That would give me something to listen to besides Raymond and Kim.

Mike knocked on our door at six thirty. "Hi, Dan," he said. He laughed and shook hands with me. "It's a great day for camping."

"Mmm," I said. Mike is a good guy, but nobody should be that happy at six thirty in the morning.

"Are you ready to go?" he asked me.

"Not really," I said.

Mom tapped me on top of my head. "He's ready," she said.

"We could make room for you," Mike told Mom.

"Not this time," Mom said.

I looked up at her. "You hate camping too, don't you?"

Mom smiled, but she didn't answer. But I knew I was right.

When she bent over to kiss me good-bye, I whispered, "It's true, isn't it? You hate camping as much as I do."

She kissed me and whispered, "Be a good sport. It's only for one night."

I left the two of them and took my bag out to the car. Kim was in the front seat. She leaned out the window and waved to me. "This is going to be so much fun," she called.

Well, at least somebody thought so.

Raymond was in the back seat. He was reading a book called *Space Explorers*. He didn't look up when I opened the door. He's

my age, but he's a lot smaller than I am. He seems older, though. About a hundred years older.

"Hi, Raymond," I said.

Raymond waved a finger. But he kept his eyes on his book.

"You know what?" Kim said. "I'm going to cook a special dinner for all of us tonight. It's called One-Pot Surprise."

"This must be our lucky day," Raymond grumbled.

"Raymond's being a grouch," Kim said. "He doesn't want to go camping."

"Who does?" I said.

"I do," she said. "I love camping. I go all the time with my Camp Fire group. If you need any help, just ask me."

"You know why we have to do this?" Raymond said. He kept looking at his book. "My dad wants us all to be friends. He wants us to be one big happy family."

"Don't get mad at me," I said. "This wasn't my idea. I hate camping."

"That's because you don't know any better," Kim said. "It's lots of fun. I love to sit by the fire and look at the stars."

"I'd rather sit by the TV and look at cartoons," I said.

Raymond looked over at me. "You still watch cartoons?"

"Sometimes. What's wrong with that?" I said.

"Nothing—if you're in preschool."

12

He turned away and started reading again.

I felt like pushing the book into his face. But I didn't. I didn't want to get in a fight before we even left home. But Raymond was asking for it.

"I used to watch cartoons," Kim said.

"You still watch cartoons," Raymond said. "Cartoons and 'Sesame Street.' "

"I do not," Kim said.

"Yes, you do." Raymond turned to me. "You ought to see her. She sits in front of the TV and sings the A-B-C song."

Kim stuck out her tongue, then turned away.

Raymond started to read his book again. I took my tape player out of my bag and put on the earphones. I popped in a cassette and leaned back in the seat.

Raymond poked me. "I can still hear that stupid music," he said.

I smiled at him. "This must be your lucky day."

Mom and Mike came walking up to the car. Kim rolled down her window and gave Mom a kiss. Raymond gave her his one-finger wave. "I know you guys are going to have a great time," Mom said.

That was easy for her to say. She was going back to our quiet apartment with her soft bed and the TV—and no Kim and Raymond.

Chapter 3

"Look," Kim yelled, "it's Star World!"

I opened my eyes and yawned. I had been asleep awhile. "Where?"

Kim pointed. "Over there. You can see the top of the roller coaster."

I spotted the roller coaster and the Ferris wheel and the big slide.

"Can we stop for a little while?" Kim asked Mike. "Please."

"It's not open yet," Mike said. "And we have better things to do."

Raymond set his book aside. "Come on, Dad. There's a campground right next door.

We could camp there and spend fourteen hours at Star World. It doesn't close until midnight."

Mike laughed. "That's not what I call a camping trip."

"Let's vote," Raymond said.

"Fine," Mike said. "But the driver gets four votes. And I vote for Baker Lake."

"Come on, Dad," Raymond said.

"We're going to Baker Lake," Mike said. "End of discussion."

I looked over at Raymond. He had really

surprised me. "Hey," I said, "I didn't know you liked Star World."

He looked at me and almost smiled. Almost. "One night I rode on the roller coaster twelve times in a row."

I had only been on the roller coaster once. It scared me a little. But I didn't say that to Raymond. "I like the bumper cars too," I said. "And the train."

"The train?" Raymond said. "You ride the train with all the babies? Do you ride the merry-go-round too? Or is that too scary for you?"

I held up my fist. "You're asking for it," I whispered.

"I'm joking," Raymond said. "Are you going to hit me just because you don't like my jokes?"

"Maybe," I said. I put on my earphones again.

"Let's play a game," Kim said later.

"Let's not," Raymond said.

"Good idea," her father said.

"Bad idea," Raymond muttered.

"Let's play I'm Going Camping," Kim said. "We did that with the Camp Fire. It's easy. The first person says, 'I'm going camping, and I'm going to take—' Then he names something that starts with the letter *A*. Then the next person says that thing and something that starts with *B*."

"This game may be too hard for Dan," Raymond said.

"You're really asking for it," I said.

"That's enough, Ray," his dad said.

"Come on," Raymond said. "It was just a joke."

"I'll start," Kim said. "I'm going camping, and I'm going to take an axe."

"I'm going camping," Mike said. "And I'm going to take an axe and a boat."

Kim pointed at me. "I'm going camping," I said. "And I'm going to take an axe and a boat and a chair."

Raymond yawned. Then he said, "I'm going camping, and I'm going to take an axe, a boat, a chair, and a diplodocus."

"That's not fair," Kim said. "I don't know what that is."

"It's not my fault you're dumb," Raymond said.

"Make him play right," Kim said.

"A diplodocus is a kind of dinosaur," Mike told her.

"But that's not fair," she said. "You have to pick something that you'd really take camping."

"I'd take a diplodocus if I had one," Raymond said. "I'd let it sleep in my tent and keep me warm."

That was the end of that game.

A little later, Kim wanted to sing. Nobody else wanted to. "I have some great songs I learned at camp," she said.

"I'd like to hear them," Mike said.

"I wouldn't," Raymond said. He put his fingers in his ears.

But Kim went ahead and sang. She sang a long song about three lambs. And a longer one about worms. And a *really* long one called "On Top of Spaghetti."

"You'd better rest your voice," Mike told her.

"I'm fine," Kim said. She went on with "Itsy-Bitsy Spider."

Raymond leaned over and whispered in my ear, "See how lucky you are not to have a sister?"

When Kim started "Found a Peanut," I put on my earphones and went to sleep.

When I woke up a half hour later, she was still singing.

Chapter 4

"We're here," Kim yelled.

I sat up and looked around. We were driving beside Baker Lake. It was a big lake. Boats out in the middle looked like toys. The water looked deep and cold.

Kim bounced up and down in the seat. "Let's go swimming right away," she shouted.

"Hey," Raymond whispered to me, "did you know that there's an alligator in this lake?"

"What?"

He leaned close to me. "A kid had a baby

alligator, and he let it go up here. The alligator's been living here ever since. It's about ten feet long now."

I looked at him. "Really?"

"Don't tell Kim about it," he whispered. "She'd be too scared to go in the water."

I looked out the window at the lake. I didn't know if Raymond was telling the truth or not. I hoped he was lying.

Mike stopped the car at a drive-up booth. He rolled down his window and paid the ranger. "Look at this," Mike told us. On the side of the booth was a big map. Every road on the map made crazy turns. Mike pointed to a spot right in the corner of the map. "That's our campsite," he said. "I picked it because it's out of the way. It should be quiet there."

I didn't want a quiet place. I wanted lots of people around.

"Please don't feed the animals," the ranger said. "And be sure to lock up your

food at night. We want our animals to work for their food."

"What kind of animals do you have?" Kim asked.

"Squirrels and chipmunks mostly," the ranger said. "Deer and raccoons at night."

"What about bears?" I asked.

The ranger smiled. "They're around here. But we don't see them very often."

"I know how we can see one," Raymond said to me. "We can put honey all over Kim's sleeping bag."

Mike drove down a crooked road and then another and another. We passed lots of tents and trailers. I felt better. I liked having other campers close by.

When Mike parked at our campsite, Kim threw open the door and jumped out. "This is perfect," she said.

I didn't know what she meant. The only thing there was a wooden picnic table.

Mike looked back at Raymond and me.

"All right," he said. "The book and the tape player stay in the car."

"Come on, Dad," Raymond said. "That's not fair."

Mike got out of the car and stretched. "From now on, you can listen to bird songs and the wind in the trees. And you can read nature."

"And we can get bored to death," Raymond said.

Raymond and I climbed out of the car. "Smell the air," Kim said.

"You kids can put up tents if you want," Mike said. "I'm going to sleep out under the stars."

"I'm going to put up my tent," Kim said. She opened the trunk and got out a green plastic bag.

I looked at Raymond. I didn't want to sleep under the stars. Not with bears around there. But I didn't want to say so.

"Let's put up a tent," Raymond said.

"If you want to, it's okay with me," I said.

Mike took a big canvas bag out of the trunk. "Here's your tent, boys. I'm going to take a look around. If you need help with the tent, ask Kim."

"We can do it," Raymond said.

After Mike left, I opened the bag. Inside were stakes and ropes and poles and a folded-up tent. "How do we do this?" I asked Raymond.

"We can figure it out," he said.

We pulled the tent out of the bag. It looked like a big wrinkled-up raincoat. We stretched it out. Then it looked like an even bigger wrinkled-up raincoat. "Is this the floor or the roof?" I asked.

"Don't rush me," Raymond said.

"My tent's all set," Kim called. "Do you need some help?"

"Yes," I said.

"No," Raymond said.

Kim sat down at the picnic table and watched us. She was smiling.

Raymond took an aluminum pole out of the bag. "It can't be very hard," he said. "There's just this one pole to hold it up."

I found a zipper on the tent. "This must be the door," I said.

"You don't call it a door," Raymond said.

"What do you call it, then?"

Raymond thought a second. "You call it the opening," he said.

I unzipped the opening, and Raymond reached inside and used the pole to push up the middle.

"I think I've found the floor," I told him.

Raymond looked back at me. "What do you mean?"

"This blue part must be the floor," I said. "But it's our roof."

Once we had the blue part on the bottom, Raymond crawled inside and lifted the roof. Then the roof fell on top of him.

The next time he raised the roof, it stayed up. Raymond crawled out of the opening. "How does it look?" he asked.

"It's a little crooked," I said. The tent was leaning to the left.

Raymond reached in and fixed it. When he was finished, the tent was leaning to the right.

Raymond stepped back from the tent. "It doesn't have to be perfect," he said.

Then the tent fell down again.

Kim didn't say a word. But her smile got bigger and bigger.

"Maybe we should ask Kim for help," I said to Raymond.

"I'm not going to ask her anything," he said. "She'd never let us forget it."

"But we need help," I said.

"We can figure it out," he said.

He reached inside and lifted up the roof again. "I've got it now," he said. But when he stepped back, the tent came crashing down.

"I think we need help," I said.

Raymond kicked the tent. "We can do it," he said. "But I have to go to the bathroom first." He went off down the road.

That was his way. He wouldn't ask for help. But I was supposed to ask while he was gone.

Chapter 5

After Raymond left, I looked at Kim. "Kim," I said, "would you help me, please?"

"Sure." She laughed and ran over to our tent. "You have to put in the stakes first."

She knew exactly what to do. I watched her stretch out the tent and hammer in stakes. Then she used the pole to lift up the middle. We were done in no time.

"It's easy once you know how," Kim said.

"Thanks, Kim," I said. "Raymond said we could figure it out. But I think it would have taken us about two years."

"Sometimes he can be so dumb," Kim said. "You know what he did today? He tried to scare me by saying there was an alligator in the lake."

I looked at her. "An alligator?"

"He told me this stupid story that couldn't fool a three-year-old. He said some kid lost his pet alligator up here, and it grew into a monster. And he thought I'd fall for that. Isn't that dumb?"

I couldn't keep from smiling. "Yeah," I said. "That's really dumb." I looked at our tent. It gave me an idea. "Let's take down the tent," I said. "I want to play a joke on Raymond."

Kim helped me take it down. Then she hid behind some trees.

Pretty soon Raymond came back. "Hey, Raymond," I said, "I think I know how to do this now. Come and help me."

"Let's wait until Dad comes back," Raymond said. "He'll show us how."

"Let's give it one more try," I said. We stretched out the tent. I hammered in the stakes just the way Kim did. Then I used the pole to lift up the middle.

Raymond stepped back and looked at the tent. "It's straight up and down," he said. "How'd you figure it out?"

"It wasn't that hard," I said.

Kim came out from behind the trees. "You got your tent up," she said.

"No problem," Raymond said. "I told you we didn't need any help."

Kim turned away and laughed.

"Hey, Raymond," I said, "you know that alligator you told me about?"

He started to smile. "Yeah?"

"We don't have to worry about it anymore."

"Why not?"

"Because the sharks ate it."

Raymond smiled and shook his head. "It was just a joke," he said. "I knew you wouldn't fall for it. Some guys do, though."

"Dumb ones," I said.

Raymond went to the car and got a book. "Dad said no books," Kim told him.

"No, he didn't," Raymond said. "He said my book stayed in the car. This isn't the same book."

But when Mike came back, Raymond hid his book under the picnic table.

"Let's go swimming before we eat lunch," Mike said.

"Good," Kim said. "That's more fun than reading a dumb book."

"Thanks for telling on me," Raymond said.

Kim smiled. "I didn't tell. I didn't use your name."

"Go into your tents and put on your swimsuits," Mike said.

After Raymond put on his swimsuit, he wrapped a towel around his shoulders. "All my ribs stick out," he said.

"Don't feel bad," I told him. "Everybody looks funny in a swimsuit."

"So you think I look funny?" he snapped. "Thanks a lot."

"That's not what I said."

Raymond glared at me. "I'll tell you one thing, Dan. I don't look half as funny as you do."

That's what I got for trying to be nice.

We walked down the road to the lake. I didn't really want to go swimming. I didn't like swimming in lakes. I liked swimming pools better. In a pool, you have steps to help you get in. And signs to tell you how deep the water is. And a nice hard bottom to stand on.

The lake water was cold, and the bottom was muddy. The mud oozed up between my toes. Mike ran into the water and started swimming. Kim went in slowly. "It's freezing," she said. But as soon as she was in, she was yelling, "Come on in. It's great."

Raymond and I stood where we were and watched. The water was up to our ankles. "Let's go in," Raymond said. "I'll race you." He took a step forward.

I went running into the water. I jumped in and started to swim. The water was so cold it made my skin hurt. I looked for Raymond, but I couldn't see him.

Then I looked back at the shore. Raymond was standing in the same place. He was

laughing at me. "You won the race," he said.

But I didn't care. It was fun to be swimming. And I didn't have to creep in, an inch at a time, the way Raymond finally did.

I didn't think about the alligator at all. Except once, when Mike grabbed my ankle.

Chapter 6

After our swim, we ate lunch. Mom had put my sandwich and apple in a paper bag. When I took out the sandwich, a note fell out. I opened the note and read it:

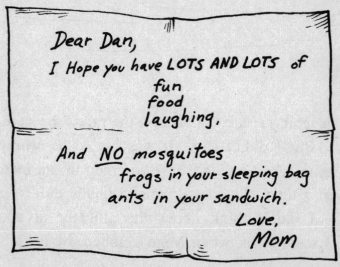

Dear Dan,
I Hope you have LOTS AND LOTS of
fun
food
laughing.

And NO mosquitoes
frogs in your sleeping bag
ants in your sandwich.
Love,
Mom

"What's that?" Raymond asked.

"Just a note," I said.

"Your mommy put a note in your lunch?" Raymond started laughing like crazy.

"That's enough, Ray," Mike said.

Raymond kept laughing. "I can't help it. A note from his mommy."

"I think it's a great idea," Mike said. "I'm going to start putting notes in your lunch. Starting right now." He pretended to write. "My dearest Raymond. I love you very much. You are such a cute little boy."

Raymond stopped laughing. "Cut it out, Dad."

"I'm just getting started," Mike said. "You have such cute little ears."

"Cut it out," Raymond said.

Now Kim was laughing like crazy. "Don't stop, Dad."

Mike turned to her. "What about you? Do you need a note too? Dearest Kimmy. I just love your cute little nose."

Kim stopped laughing right away. "All right, Dad," she said.

Nobody talked about notes after that. But I was still mad. I didn't see anything funny about Mom writing me a note.

After lunch we rented canoes. We had to put on life jackets before we got in. The jackets were fat and hot. I dipped mine in the water first, then put it on.

Everyone did that after I did. "Good idea," Mike said.

"That's better," Kim said.

Even Raymond said, "Yeah."

Mike and Kim took one canoe, and Ray-

mond and I took the other. "You're bigger," Raymond said. "You sit in the front."

I didn't understand that. But I sat in front.

Mike pushed our canoe away from the dock. "Paddle together," he said. "One on each side. That way, your canoe will go straight."

It seemed easy, but it wasn't. Our canoe went right, then left. Then right again. And sometimes it went in a circle.

Mike and Kim went past us. "Bye-bye," Kim called. "See ya."

"Why's Mike in the back?" I asked Raymond. "I thought the big person sat in front."

"He's doing it wrong," Raymond said.

I watched their canoe get smaller and smaller. "He doesn't look like he's doing it wrong."

Pretty soon I figured out why Raymond wanted to be in the back. That way, he could stop paddling for a while, and I wouldn't know it. Whenever I'd look back and catch him, he'd say, "I'm just changing hands."

We paddled along the shore of the lake for a long time. When I looked back, I couldn't see the campground.

"I'm tired," I said finally. I put my paddle in the canoe.

Raymond stopped paddling. "I guess we can rest awhile if you want."

I was too tired to answer that.

We sat for a few minutes. I reached over the side and scooped up some water to dribble on my head and neck.

"Look," Raymond said. "On the shore."

"Where?"

He pointed. "There. See the brown thing?"

I saw something move. "What is it?"

"I think it's a beaver. Let's get closer."

We paddled slowly toward the shore, trying not to make a sound. "It's a beaver, all right," I whispered.

"Shh," Raymond said.

The beaver raised its head. Then it zipped down the bank, like a kid on a slide. It slipped into the water with only a tiny splash. Then it smacked the water with its tail. That sounded like a firecracker.

Raymond and I looked at each other. We both said, "Wow" at the same time.

I kept my eyes on the water. "It has to come up pretty soon," I said.

"No, it doesn't," Raymond said. "Beavers can stay underwater for fifteen minutes."

I looked back at him. "How do you know that?"

"I read books," he said. "You ought to try it sometime."

In a few minutes, Mike and Kim came paddling back. "I didn't know where you were," Mike said.

"We saw a beaver," Raymond said.

"Oh, sure," Kim said. "Did you see an alligator too?"

"We really did," I told her. "It was on that bank."

Kim shook her head. "Maybe. Maybe not."

"You were lucky," Mike said. "Beavers do most of their work at night."

We paddled up to the bank and looked around. We didn't see the beaver again. But we did see a tree that had been chewed.

"Take a look, Kim," Raymond said. "Do you think Dan and I chewed that tree?"

Kim barely looked at the tree. "Maybe they didn't really see a beaver," she told her father. "They could have seen the tree and made up the rest."

On the way back, I saw a fish swimming along. "Look," I said. "It's a big fish." I leaned over the side to get a better look.

"I see it," Raymond yelled, leaning the same way.

I felt the canoe begin to tip. "Look out!" I shouted. I quickly leaned the other way.

That might have worked, but Raymond did the same thing. The canoe tipped in the other direction and dumped us into the lake. The water was freezing.

The life jacket brought me to the top of the water. I ended up right next to the canoe. Raymond came up spitting water. "Nice going, stupid," he yelled.

"It wasn't all my fault," I said. "You leaned over too."

Mike and Kim paddled back toward us. Kim was laughing. "Swim your canoe over to the shore," Mike said. "You can get in easier that way."

Swimming in a life jacket was hard. It

took us a long time to get the canoe to shore.

"That was so dumb," Raymond said.

"It wasn't all my fault," I said again.

He looked at me and shook his head. "If you try to blame me, you're even dumber than you look."

That was too much. I walked over and gave him a shove.

Raymond just stood there. "I'm not going to fight you."

I pushed him again. "What's the matter? Are you scared?"

"What's the point of fighting?" he said. "You're bigger than I am. I know you can beat me up."

"Kim could probably beat you up," I said.

"Hit me if you want," he said. "I'll just stand here."

I thought about hitting him. But I didn't.

"I never fight," he said. "Fighting is stupid."

"You fight all the time," I said. "You just fight with your mouth."

Raymond smiled. "Nobody gets hurt that way."

"Yes, they do," I said. "I'd rather have you hit me than call me names."

Raymond looked surprised. "Really?"

I was still mad, but I didn't know what else to say. Finally I said, "Let's go back."

Raymond climbed into the canoe. "I still don't think it was my fault the canoe tipped over," he said.

I didn't get into the canoe. I pushed it away from shore. Then I reached out and tipped it over. Raymond plopped into the lake.

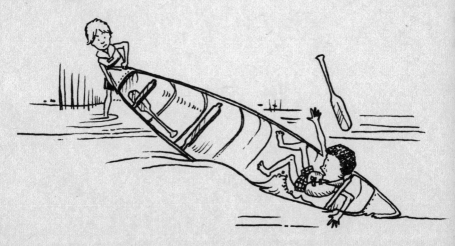

He came up spitting water again. "What's the matter with you?"

"That time it was all my fault," I said.

Raymond looked at me and almost laughed. Almost.

Chapter 7

Later we took a walk around the lake. Kim kept walking ahead of us. She had her camera, and she was hoping to get a picture of a beaver.

We found some more trees that the beavers had chewed. We saw a dam the beavers had made. But we didn't see any beavers.

Kim took pictures of the chewed trees. "I don't see how beavers do it," she said. "You'd think they'd get full of wood and wear out their teeth."

"Their teeth keep growing all their lives," Raymond told her. "And they pull their lips closed behind their front teeth, so they don't swallow the wood at all. That's how they can chew stuff underwater without drowning."

Raymond could be interesting when he wasn't being a pain. But that didn't happen very often.

On the way back, we had to stop and rest. "This isn't a vacation," Raymond said. "This is work."

Mike laughed. "Today is a warm-up. Tomorrow we'll take a five-mile hike."

I looked at Raymond. Raymond looked at me. We shook our heads.

"That's not so far," Kim said. "My Camp Fire group went on a six-mile hike."

"It isn't as bad as it sounds," Mike said. "We won't do it all at once. It's a little over two miles to Baker Falls. We'll go swimming there and have a picnic before we walk back."

That sounded better. But it still didn't sound good.

After our walk, we swam in the lake again. Then Kim began to cook supper on our camp stove. She was making One-Pot Surprise. She opened six cans and two boxes. Then she dumped everything into the pot and stirred.

I walked by the stove and glanced at the One-Pot Surprise. It looked like a surprise. But it didn't look like a good surprise.

"I have some candy bars in our tent," Raymond told me. "We may need them."

"Time for dinner," Kim called. Mike got drinks out of the ice chest. I took a bottle of orange pop. That was one of the few good things about camping—orange pop for dinner.

Kim put a big mound of One-Pot Surprise on my plate.

I looked at my mound. I could see noodles in it. And peas and carrots. And beans. And something red. I took a small bite.

"How is it?" Kim asked me.

It was terrible. It tasted like oatmeal.

Lumpy oatmeal with beans. But Kim was smiling and happy, and I wanted her to stay that way. She might be a terrible cook, but she *had* helped me with the tent when I needed it. "It's good," I said.

"I like it," Mike said. But he ate very slowly. Later on, he got up to get another drink and came back with an empty plate. So I knew he'd dumped his One-Pot Surprise in the bushes.

Raymond didn't say anything. He just held his stomach and made faces when Kim wasn't looking.

I cleaned my plate. I took big bites, then washed them down with orange pop.

Kim had seconds. "I love this stuff," she said. She brought the pot over to me. "Here. Have some more, Dan. I saved some for you."

"Thank you," I said.

"This is your lucky day," Raymond said.

While we ate, we could hear the noises from other campsites. Some people had radios, and some had TVs.

"People are crazy," Mike said. "They go camping and bring their TV."

That didn't sound crazy to me at all. It would have been nice to curl up in my sleeping bag and watch a little TV—just the way I did at home sometimes.

After dinner we went to a ranger talk. The talk was all right, but she made us sing stupid songs first. Then she showed slides of animals and flowers. She showed pictures of beavers and the beaver dam. "Anybody who walks around the west side of the lake can see the dam," she said. "But only a few lucky people will see the beavers."

Raymond hit me with his elbow. "See?" he said. "We're special."

The ranger also showed pictures of bears. They were good pictures, but they gave me the creeps. I wondered if Mike would let me sleep in the car. That was the only safe place.

It was almost dark when we got back to our campsite. We roasted marshmallows over the camp stove. I wished we could have a real fire, but that was against the park rules.

"We need a ghost story," Kim said.

I didn't think we did. But I couldn't say so.

"I don't know a ghost story," Mike said. "But I did hear a creepy story the other day."

"Tell it," Kim said.

"Go ahead, Dad," Raymond said.

I didn't say a word.

Mike told a story about a man who rented a house. One night the man felt something next to him in bed. It turned out to be a big pet snake that belonged to the people who lived there before.

While Mike told the story, Kim kept going, "Ooo." Raymond kept saying, "I know what it is."

The story didn't scare me. But it didn't make me want to go to bed either.

Then we went to the rest rooms to brush our teeth. We walked past all the tents and trailers. Some of them were dark and quiet. At one picnic table, people were playing cards with a lantern for light. In one trailer, a TV was on.

"We should have camped closer to the rest rooms," Raymond complained.

"I love walking at night," Mike said. "Turn off your flashlights for a minute and just listen."

"I can hear in the light," Raymond said.

"Turn them off," Mike said.

We stopped walking and turned off our lights. Everything seemed really dark. I looked around and saw lights from some of the camps.

"Now listen," Mike said. "Hear the wind in the pines? And the crickets? And you'll hear birds sometimes."

I heard the wind and the crickets. I also heard some woman say, "Charlie, where did you put the ice chest?"

"It's like a different world," Mike said.

We turned on our lights and started to walk. "You know what I heard?" Raymond whispered to me. "I heard my stomach say it didn't want any more One-Pot Surprise."

Chapter 8

I really wanted to sleep in the car. But if I said so, Kim and Raymond would know I was scared. So I got into the tent. But if I heard any bear noises, I was heading for the car right away.

Once I got into my sleeping bag, I felt like talking. Even to Raymond. I wasn't really scared. But I didn't want to lie there and listen for bears.

Raymond didn't want to talk. He had a book and his flashlight. He got down in his sleeping bag and covered his head. He didn't want his dad to see the light.

I lay on my back and listened. Nothing sounded right. I was used to city sounds. Cars and trucks and banging doors. Not wind in the trees and crickets.

Then I heard some clumps and thumps. I tried to think about baseball or TV. Or even school. But I kept thinking of newspapers with big headlines:

BEAR EATS CAMPERS.

I felt the tent shake. I knew it was the wind. But I kept seeing headlines:

EARTHQUAKE WRECKS CAMPGROUND.

I tried not to think about Mike's story. But soon I saw the headline:

SNAKE SWALLOWS CAMPER.

I wished I had my radio. I wished Raymond would quit reading and talk to me. Mostly, I wished I was home in my own bed.

61

I must have fallen asleep for a while. The next thing I remember is waking up fast. I sat straight up. I didn't know where I was. Then I felt my sleeping bag on the hard ground and remembered.

I heard a growl. It was just outside the tent.

Raymond poked me. "Dan, Dan, do you hear that?"

"I hear it," I said. I was glad he was awake too.

"What do you think it is?" he asked.

I listened. It was a deep, loud growl, then a moaning sound. Then a growl again. I figured it was a bear. But I didn't want to say that. "I don't know."

"You'd better take a look," he said.

"Me? Why me?"

"You're closer to the opening."

"I can move and let you by," I said.

"Just open it a little and take a look." He tried to hand me his flashlight.

"I have my flashlight," I said. I took my light from under my pillow. "But maybe we should wait and see if it'll leave. We don't want to make it mad."

"Go ahead," Raymond said. "Unzip the tent."

I listened to the growl again. It seemed even louder.

"Go on," Raymond said.

I reached out and unzipped the tent an inch. The zipper made a lot of noise. I pulled back my hand and waited. Then I unzipped the tent another inch. Then another. The growl stopped for a minute, then started again.

"That's far enough," Raymond said. "You can look out now."

"You can look if you want," I said.

"You do it, Dan."

I waited for a minute. I was scared. But I wanted to see what was making the noise. I poked my flashlight through the hole. I got my eye next to the flashlight. Then I turned on the switch.

I couldn't see anything. Just the picnic table. And Mike's sleeping bag. I moved the light around.

I heard the growl again. It sounded as if it was coming from the sleeping bag. I moved my light that way. Mike was lying on his back with his mouth open. He was snoring.

"What is it?" Raymond whispered.

"It's a big bear," I said. "Big as the car."

Raymond slid down in his sleeping bag. "Really?"

"No," I said. "It's your dad. He's snoring."

Raymond shook his head and smiled. "Dad doesn't snore."

"Well," I said, "I don't think he's singing."

We lay there and listened to the snoring. "He sounds like a pig grunting," Raymond said.

We tried to make snoring sounds like Mike's, and we ended up laughing.

"Hey, Dan," Raymond said, "as long as we're awake, let's go to the bathroom."

"It's too far."

"Come on. Let's go."

I unzipped the opening. "You want to go down there in our pajamas?" I asked.

"Sure. Everybody's asleep."

We pulled on our shoes and crawled out

of the tent. Mike was still snoring. We tip-toed past his sleeping bag. "I wish I had a tape recorder," Raymond whispered.

We walked down the road to the bath-room. The whole camp was dark and quiet. Raymond kept shining his light around.

On the way back, Raymond stopped and grabbed my arm. "Dan," he whispered, "look over there."

I looked that way. Two eyes were shining in the light. "What is it?" I whispered. All I could see was a dark shape. A big dark shape.

"I don't know," Raymond said. He started to back up. I did the same.

The animal started toward us. We moved back faster. The eyes got bigger. And I could hear galloping footsteps.

"Run!" Raymond said. He turned and raced away. His light flopped up and down.

I ran after him. I could still hear the animal behind us. It was breathing hard.

I ran past Raymond. He was also breath-

ing hard. "Keep going," I said. "Don't stop!"

Then Raymond tripped and fell. "Help!" he called. "It's got me!"

Chapter 9

I stopped and shone my light behind me. Raymond was lying on the ground. "Help me!" he yelled. The dark animal was on top of him.

I wanted to keep running. I wanted to get miles away.

But I couldn't do that. I turned and ran back. I tried to keep my light on Raymond, but it bounced up and down when I ran. The animal's eyes flashed in my light.

I stopped just in front of Raymond. He was curled into a ball with his face in the dirt.

I started to laugh. The animal was a big
black dog. It was licking Raymond's neck
and wagging its tail. Its tongue was about a
foot long.

"It's okay, Raymond," I said, trying to
stop laughing. "It's just a dog. And it likes
you."

Raymond groaned and sat up. He shoved
the dog away. "It's not funny," he said.

The dog jumped off Raymond and ran to me. It started licking me with its foot-long tongue. "Go on," I said.

Raymond got to his feet. "A dumb dog," he said. He slapped at the dirt on his pajamas. "No one is supposed to have dogs in a campground."

"Are you okay?" I asked him.

"What do you think?" he said. "I've got dirt in my mouth, dirt up my nose, dirt all over my pajamas. And I just about had a heart attack."

I pushed the dog away. "I was scared too."

By then, people started coming out of their tents. "I heard somebody call for help," a man said.

"Is everything all right out there?" someone else yelled.

"Let's get out of here," Raymond whispered. We hurried down the road.

"Somebody's in trouble," a man shouted.

"Everything's okay," I called back.

The dog went running toward a tent.

"What happened?" somebody else asked.

"Let's go," Raymond whispered.

We turned off our flashlights and sneaked away.

We didn't stop until everything around us was quiet. All the tents and trailers were dark. Raymond brushed at his pajamas again. "I'm glad we got out of there," he said. "I didn't feel like telling the whole world that a dumb dog scared us."

"I know," I said.

"I still have dirt in my nose," Raymond said.

I looked around at the dark tents. "Hey, Raymond," I said, "do you know where we are?"

"Sort of," he said. "Don't you?"

I looked down the dark road. Then I turned and looked up the road. "I'm not sure."

"What's the number of our campsite?"

"I didn't even look at the number," I said.

"Me neither," he said. "But I think our camp's this way."

We went down a road. Then another one. And another. None of them looked like any road I'd seen before. I felt a cold chill run down my back.

"This is really stupid," Raymond said. "What'll we do?"

"Let's ask somebody to help us," I said.

"Do you really want to do that?" he asked. "We're in our dumb pajamas. Do you want to wake up somebody and say we're lost right here in the middle of the stupid campground?"

I did—sort of. But I said, "No."

"This is really stupid," he said again. "Let's see. We left the rest room, and then we went down that road. Then we turned—" He shook his head. "This is really stupid."

"Let's try this road," I said. We went down the road and ended up on another road. I had the feeling we'd been there before. About ten minutes before. "We could ask somebody," I said. "I don't care what they think."

"We're going to look so stupid," Raymond said. "Getting lost in the dumb campground. We couldn't find our way back from the potty."

I shone my light down another road. I saw an EXIT arrow on a tree. "Hey," I said, "we can follow the arrows to the exit."

Raymond shook his head. "Then what?"

"There's a map there, remember? Your dad showed us our campsite on the map. It was right in the corner."

"Yeah." Raymond banged me on the back. "Let's go." He headed down the road. He was almost running.

At the entrance booth, we looked at the map. We found the campsite in the corner.

It was number 64. "I wish I had something to write on," Raymond said.

"Don't worry," I told him. "I won't forget that number in a hundred years."

We stood at the map and counted the roads so we could find our way to Campsite 64. Then we counted them again just to be sure.

It was easy after that. In five minutes, we were walking into our campsite.

Everything would have been fine except that Kim and Mike were standing by the table. "Where have you been?" Kim called out.

"What are you guys doing up?" Raymond asked.

"I got worried about you two," Mike said. "You were gone a long time. And Kim heard me moving around and thought I was fixing breakfast."

"What were you doing?" Kim asked. "We even went down to the rest rooms looking for you."

I waited for Raymond to say something. But he didn't say a word. "We just felt like taking a walk in the moonlight," I said.

"We were listening to the wind in the trees," Raymond said.

"And the crickets and the birds," I said. "All kinds of birds."

"It's like a different world," Raymond went on.

"You probably got lost," Kim said.

"In the campground?" Raymond said. "Give me a break."

Chapter 10

Raymond and I got into our tent. I zipped the flap. Then we started to laugh. But we had to hold our hands over our mouths so Mike and Kim wouldn't hear.

"That stupid dog," Raymond whispered after awhile. "I thought it was a bear."

I thought of that dog and its foot-long tongue, and I started to laugh again.

Raymond reached into his bag and got some candy bars. "Have one," he said.

We sat on our sleeping bags and ate the candy bars. Outside I could hear the wind in the trees. And crickets. And birds.

"We'd better have another candy bar,"

Raymond said. "We have to go on a five-mile hike in the morning."

"No problem," I said. "I think we went five miles tonight."

And we started to laugh again.

I was almost asleep when Raymond poked me. "Dan. Hey, Dan."

I moaned. "Don't tell me you have to go to the bathroom again."

"I've been thinking about something."

"Me too. I was thinking about sleep."

"Come on, Dan. This is important. I think we can get my dad to stop at Star World on the way home."

"Really?"

"We can do it if we handle things just right," he said. "First we have to get Kim on our side. We want her to ask my dad."

"I'll talk to her in the morning," I said.

"You never had a sister, did you?" he said. "You can't do things that way."

"What do you mean?"

"If we ask Kim to do something, she'll say no—just because we asked her. If it wasn't her idea, she won't like it. So we won't ask her."

"But if we don't ask her, then how—?"

Raymond put his hand on my arm. "Tomorrow you and I will start talking about the roller coaster. And we'll tell her she's too young and too little to ride on it. That'll make her mad. See what I'm saying?"

I started to laugh. "Yeah, I see."

"Then she'll want to show us she isn't too little," Raymond went on. "And she'll think going to Star World was *her* idea."

At breakfast the next morning, Raymond, Kim, and I were eating cornflakes and bananas. Mike had gone to the rest rooms to shave. Raymond elbowed me. I knew what he wanted. I was supposed to start talking about the roller coaster. But I didn't know how to get started. How do you get from cornflakes to roller coasters?

Finally Raymond said, "I had a dream last night. I dreamed I was riding a roller coaster."

"I had a dream too," Kim said. "I dreamed two boys got lost in the campground."

Raymond elbowed me again. "I like roller coasters," I said. "I used to be afraid of them when I was little, but I like them now."

"Lots of little kids are afraid to ride them," Raymond said. "Especially girls."

Kim got up from the table. "Dan," she said, "will you come with me for a minute?"

"Sure."

We walked down the road past the next camp. Then Kim stopped and said, "I know what Raymond's doing. He wants to stop at Star World on the way home, doesn't he?"

"I think so."

"I know so," Kim said. "And he's afraid to ask Dad. So he's trying to get me to do it."

"Oh," I said. I didn't know what else to say.

"He's so stupid," she said. "Why doesn't he just ask me?" She looked at me and smiled. "If we get back from our hike in time, I think it'd be neat to go to Star World. I'll go ask Dad right now. I'm not afraid." She went down the road to meet Mike.

"Did my trick work?" Raymond asked me when I came back.

"Well," I said, "she's going to ask your dad if we can stop at Star World."

Raymond smiled. "See? You have to know how to do these things."

I laughed to myself. Raymond knew a lot of things I didn't, but there were other things he didn't have a clue about.

We had a good day. On our hike, we saw an old mine and lots of deer. We swam at the pool beneath the waterfall. It was fun to swim under the falls and let the water land on our heads.

And that afternoon, on our way home, we stopped at Star World for one hour. (Mike said an hour was all he could stand.)

But in that one hour, I had:

a hot dog,
two slices of pizza,
a root beer,
a rainbow Snow-Kone,
a ride on the Ferris wheel and the
   octopus,
three rides on the bumper cars,
and four rides on the roller coaster—two
   in the front seat with Kim (Raymond
   was scared to ride in front).

And I bought a big caramel lollipop that lasted all the way home.

So I guess I don't hate camping. It can be fun—if you know how to do it.

But do me a favor. Don't tell Mom she was right.